Dad at the Park

Written by Jill Eggleton
Illustrated by Raymond McGrath

Dad and the kids
went to the park.
They like the park.

2

"I am going on this swing,"
said Dad.

"You are too big,"
said the kids.
"The swing will **crack!**"

"I am going on this rope,"
said Dad.

"You are too big,"
said the kids.
"The rope will *snap!*"

"I am going down
this slide," said Dad.

"Look at the slide,"
said the kids.
"You are too big!"

Dad looked at the slide.
"I am **not** too big,"
he said.

"I will go down the slide."

Dad went down the slide.

Whooooooooooosh!

"**Oops!**" said Dad.
"**I am stuck!**
I **am** too big."

A Map

Guide Notes

Title: Dad at the Park

Stage: Early (1) – Red

Genre: Fiction

Approach: Guided Reading

Processes: Thinking Critically, Exploring Language, Processing Information

Written and Visual Focus: Map

Word Count: 103

THINKING CRITICALLY

(sample questions)

- What do you think this story could be about?
- Look at the title and read it to the children.
- Why do you think Dad wanted to go on all the play equipment at the park?
- How do you think Dad felt when he got stuck?
- How do you think Dad will get out of the slide?
- What sorts of things do you think Dad could do with the kids?

EXPLORING LANGUAGE

Terminology

Title, cover, illustrations, author, illustrator

Vocabulary

Interest words: crack, snap, stuck, whoosh, oops

High-frequency words: they, will

Positional words: down, on

Print Conventions

Capital letter for sentence beginnings and names (**D**ad), periods, commas, quotation marks, exclamation marks